PiPPi
Goes to School

The text in this book has been excerpted, with Astrid Lindgren's assistance, from two chapters in *Pippi Longstocking*.

VIKING
Published by the Penguin Group
Penguin Putnam Inc., 375 Hudson Street, New York, New York 10014, U.S.A.
Penguin Books Ltd, 27 Wrights Lane, London W8 5TZ, England
Penguin Books Australia Ltd, Ringwood, Victoria, Australia
Penguin Books Canada Ltd, 10 Alcorn Avenue, Toronto, Ontario, Canada M4V 3B2
Penguin Books (N.Z.) Ltd, 182–190 Wairau Road, Auckland 10, New Zealand

Penguin Books Ltd, Registered Offices: Harmondsworth, Middlesex, England

This edition first published in 1998 by Viking,
a member of Penguin Putnam Books for Young Readers

3 5 7 9 10 8 6 4

Text copyright The Viking Press, Inc., 1950
Copyright renewed Viking Penguin Inc., 1978
Illustrations copyright © Michael Chesworth, 1998
All rights reserved

LIBRARY OF CONGRESS CATALOGING-IN-PUBLICATION DATA
Lindgren, Astrid, date
Pippi goes to school / by Astrid Lindgren ; illustrated by Michael
Chesworth ; translated by Frances Lamborn.
p. cm. — (A Pippi Longstocking storybook)
Summary: After Tommy and Annika entice Pippi into going to school, her
first–and–only day there is unlike anything they ever expected.
ISBN 0-670-88075-2 (hc)
[1. First day of school—Fiction. 2. Schools—Fiction.
3. Humorous stories.] I. Chesworth, Michael, ill. II. Lamborn,
Frances. III. Title. IV. Series: Lindgren, Astrid, date.
Pippi Longstocking storybook.
PZ7.L6585Pgf 1998 [E]—dc21 97-51432 CIP AC

Printed in Hong Kong
Set in New Aster

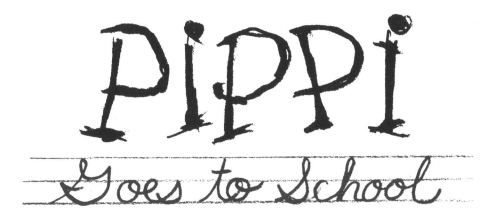

PiPPi
Goes to School

By Astrid Lindgren
Pictures by Michael Chesworth

VIKING

ay out at the end of a tiny little town was an old overgrown garden, and in the garden was an old house, and in the house lived Pippi Longstocking. She was nine years old, and she lived there all alone. She had no mother and no father, and that was of course very nice because there was no one to tell her to go to bed just when she was having the most fun, and no one who could make her take cod liver oil when she much preferred caramel candy.

Once upon a time Pippi had had a father of whom she was extremely fond. He was a sea captain who sailed on the great ocean, and Pippi had sailed with him in his ship until one day her father was blown overboard in a storm and disappeared.

But Pippi was absolutely certain he would come back.

Her father had bought the old house in the garden many years ago. While Pippi was waiting for him to come back she went straight home to live at Villa Villekulla. That was the name of the house.

Two things Pippi took with her from the ship: a little monkey whose name was Mr. Nilsson—he was a present from her father—and a big suitcase full of gold pieces. Pippi also had a horse of her own that she had bought with one of her many

gold pieces the day she came home to Villa Villekulla.

Beside Villa Villekulla was another garden and another house. In that house lived a father and mother and two charming children, Tommy and Annika, who often wished for a playmate. And when Pippi Longstocking moved next door, they got the best playmate any child could wish for. This is the story of one of their adventures together. . . .

Of course Tommy and Annika went to school. Each morning at eight o'clock they trotted off, hand in hand, swinging their schoolbags.

At that time Pippi was usually grooming her horse or dressing Mr. Nilsson in his little suit. Or else she was taking her morning exercises, which meant turning forty-three somersaults in a row.

Tommy and Annika always looked longingly toward Villa Villekulla as they started off to school. They would much rather have gone to play with Pippi. If only Pippi had been going to school too; that would have been something else.

The more they thought about it the worse they felt to think that Pippi did not go to school, and at last they determined to try to persuade her to begin.

"You can't imagine what a nice teacher we have," said Tommy artfully to Pippi one afternoon.

"If you only knew what fun it is in school!" Annika
added. "I'd die if I couldn't go to school."

Pippi was bathing her feet in a tub.

"You don't have to stay so very long," continued
Tommy. "Just until two o'clock."

"Yes, and besides, we get Christmas vacation and
Easter vacation and summer vacation," said Annika.

Pippi bit her big toe thoughtfully but still said
nothing. Suddenly, she poured all the water out on
the kitchen floor, so that Mr. Nilsson, who sat near
her playing with a mirror, got his pants absolutely
soaked.

"It's not fair!" said Pippi sternly without paying
any attention to Mr. Nilsson's puzzled air about his
wet pants. "It is absolutely unfair! I don't intend to
stand it!"

"What's the matter now?" asked Tommy.

"In four months it will be Christmas, and then you'll have Christmas vacation. But I, what'll I get?" Pippi's voice sounded sad. "No Christmas vacation, not even the tiniest bit of a Christmas vacation," she complained. "Something will have to be done about that. Tomorrow morning I'll begin school."

Tommy and Annika clapped their hands. "Hurrah! We'll wait for you outside our gate at eight o'clock."

"Oh, no," said Pippi. "I can't begin as early as that. And besides, I'm going to ride to school."

And ride she did. Exactly at ten o'clock the next

day she lifted her horse off the porch, and a little later all the people in the town ran to their windows to see what horse it was that was running away.

Pippi galloped wildly into the schoolyard, jumped
off the horse, tied him to a tree, and burst into the
schoolroom with such a noise and a clatter that

Tommy and Annika and all their classmates jumped
in their seats.

"Hi, there," cried Pippi, waving her big hat.

Tommy and Annika had told their teacher that a
new girl named Pippi Longstocking was coming, and
as she was a very pleasant teacher, she had decided

to do all she could to make Pippi happy in school.

Pippi threw herself down on a vacant bench. The teacher said in a very friendly voice, "Welcome to school, little Pippi. I hope that you will enjoy yourself here and learn a great deal."

"Yes, and I hope I'll get some Christmas vacation," said Pippi. "That is the reason I've come."

"If you would first tell me your whole name," said the teacher, "then I'll register you in school."

"My name is Pippilotta Delicatessa Windowshade Mackrelmint Efraim's Daughter Longstocking, daughter of Captain Efraim Longstocking. Pippi is really only a nickname, because Papa thought that Pippilotta was too long to say."

"Indeed?" said the teacher. "Well, then we shall call you Pippi too. But now," she continued, "suppose we test you a little and see what you know. Let us begin with arithmetic. Pippi, can you tell me what seven plus five is?"

Pippi, astonished and dismayed, looked at her and said, "Well, if you don't know that yourself, you needn't think I'm going to tell you."

All the children stared in horror at Pippi, and the teacher explained that one couldn't answer that way in school.

"I beg your pardon," said Pippi contritely. "I didn't know that. I won't do it again."

"No, let us hope not," said the teacher. "And now I will tell you that seven plus five is twelve."

"See that!" said Pippi. "You knew it yourself. Why are you asking then?"

The teacher decided to act as if nothing unusual were happening and went on with her examination.

"Well now, Pippi, how much do you think eight plus four is?"

"Oh, about sixty-seven," hazarded Pippi.

"Of course not," said the teacher. "Eight plus four is twelve."

"Well now, really," said Pippi, "that is carrying things too far. You just said that seven plus five is twelve. There should be some rhyme and reason to things even in school. Furthermore, if you are so childishly interested in that foolishness, why don't you sit down in a corner by yourself and do arithmetic and leave us alone so we can play tag?"

The teacher decided there was no point in trying to teach Pippi any more arithmetic. "Can Tommy answer this one?" she asked. "If Lisa has seven apples and Axel has nine apples, how many apples do they have together?"

"Yes, you tell, Tommy," Pippi interrupted, "and tell

me too, if Lisa gets a stomach-ache and Axel gets more stomach-ache, whose fault is it and where did they get hold of the apples in the first place?"

The teacher tried to pretend that she hadn't heard and turned to Annika. "Now, Annika, here's a problem for you: Gustav was with his schoolmates on a picnic. He had a quarter when he started out and seven cents when he got home. How much did he spend?"

"Yes, indeed," said Pippi, "and I also want to know why he was so extravagant, and if it was pop he bought, and if he washed his ears properly before he left home."

The teacher decided to give up arithmetic altogether. She thought maybe Pippi would prefer to learn to read. So she took out a pretty little card with a picture of an iguana on it. In front of the iguana's nose was the letter "i."

"Now, Pippi," she said briskly, "you'll see something nice. You see here an iguana. And the letter in front of this iguana is called *i*."

"That I'll never believe," said Pippi. "I think it looks exactly like a straight line with a little fly speck over it. But what I'd really like to know is, what has the iguana to do with the fly speck?"

The teacher took out another card with a picture of a snake on it and told Pippi that the letter on that was an *s*.

"Speaking of snakes," said Pippi, "I'll never, ever forget the time I had a fight with a huge snake in India. You can't imagine what a dreadful snake it was, fourteen yards long and mad as a hornet, and one time he came and wanted me for dessert, and he wound himself around me—uhhh!—but I've been around a bit, I said, and hit him in the head, bang, and then I hit him again, and bingo! he was dead, and, indeed, so that is the letter *s*—most remarkable!"

Pippi had to stop to get her breath. And the teacher, who had now begun to think that Pippi was an unruly and troublesome child, decided that the class should have drawing for a while. She took out paper and pencils and passed them out to the children.

"Now you may draw whatever you wish," she said and sat down at her desk and began to correct homework. In a little while she looked up to see how the drawing was going. All the children sat looking at Pippi, who lay flat on the floor, drawing to her heart's content.

"But, Pippi," said the teacher impatiently, "why in the world aren't you drawing on your paper?"

"I filled that long ago. There isn't room enough for my whole horse on that little snip of a paper," said Pippi. "Just now I'm working on his front legs, but when I get to his tail I guess I'll have to go out in the hall."

The teacher thought hard for a while. "Suppose instead we all sing a little song," she suggested.

All the children stood up by their seats except Pippi; she stayed where she was on the floor. "You go ahead and sing," she said. "I'll rest myself a while. Too much learning tires even the healthiest."

But now the teacher's patience came to an end. She told all the children to go out into the yard so she could talk to Pippi alone.

When the teacher and Pippi were alone, Pippi got up and walked to the desk. "Do you know what?" she

said. "It was awfully fun to come to school to find out what it was like. But I don't think I care about going to school any more, Christmas vacation or no Christmas vacation. There's altogether too many apples and iguanas and snakes and things like that. It makes me dizzy in the head. I hope that you, Teacher, won't be sorry."

But the teacher said she certainly was sorry, most of all because Pippi wouldn't behave decently; and that any girl who acted as badly as Pippi did

wouldn't be allowed to go to school even if she wanted to ever so much.

"Have I behaved badly?" asked Pippi, much astonished. "Goodness, I didn't know that," she added. She stood silent for a while, and then she said in a trembling voice, "You understand, Teacher, don't you, that when you have a mother who's an angel and a father who is a cannibal king, and when you have sailed on the ocean all your whole life, then you don't know just how to behave in school with all the apples and iguanas."

Then the teacher said she understood and didn't feel annoyed with Pippi any longer, and maybe Pippi could come back to school when she was a little older. Pippi positively beamed with delight. "I think you are awfully nice, Teacher. And here is something for you."

Out of her pocket Pippi took a lovely little gold watch and laid it on the desk. The teacher said she couldn't possibly accept such a valuable gift from Pippi, but Pippi replied, "You've got to take it; other-

27

wise I'll come back again tomorrow, and that would be a pretty how-do-you-do."

Then Pippi rushed out to the schoolyard and jumped on her horse. All the children gathered around to pat the horse and see her off.

"You ought to know about the schools in Argentina," said Pippi. "Easter vacation begins three days after Christmas vacation ends, and when Easter vacation is over there are three days and then it's summer vacation. Summer vacation ends on the first of November, and then you have a tough time until Christmas vacation begins on November eleventh. But you can stand that because there are at least no lessons. Arithmetic they don't have at all, and if there is any kid who knows what seven plus five is he has to stand in the corner all day—that is, if he's foolish enough to let the teacher know that he knows. They have reading on Friday, and then only if they have some books, which they never have."

"But what do they do in school?" asked one little boy.

"Eat caramels," said Pippi decidedly. "There is a long pipe that goes from a caramel factory nearby directly into the schoolroom, and caramels keep shooting out of it all day long so the children have all they can do to eat them up."

"Yes, but what does the teacher do?" asked one little girl.

"Takes the paper off the caramels for the children, of course," said Pippi. Then she waved her big hat.

"So long, kids," she cried gaily. "Now you won't see

me for a while. But always remember how many apples Axel had or you'll be sorry."

With a ringing laugh Pippi rode out through the gate so wildly that the pebbles whirled around the horse's hoofs and the windowpanes rattled in the schoolhouse.